HORRiD HENRY
Gets Rich Quick

HORRID HENRY
Gets Rich Quick

Francesca Simon
Illustrated by Tony Ross

Orion
Children's Books

Horrid Henry Gets Rich Quick originally appeared in
Horrid Henry Gets Rich Quick first published in Great Britain in 1998
by Orion Children's Books
This edition first published in Great Britain in 2010
by Orion Children's Books
This edition published in 2016 by Hodder and Stoughton

3 5 7 9 10 8 6 4

A CIP catalogue record for this book is available from the British Library.

ISBN 978 1 4440 0001 6

Printed and bound in China

The paper and board used in this book are
made from wood from responsible sources.

Orion Children's Books
An imprint of Hachette Children's Group
Part of Hodder and Stoughton
Carmelite House
50 Victoria Embankment
London EC4Y 0DZ

An Hachette UK Company
www.hachette.co.uk

www.hachettechildrens.co.uk
www.horridhenry.co.uk

For David Abell and Seann Alderking,
magical musicians, fabulous friends

Look out for . . .
Don't Be Horrid, Henry!
Horrid Henry's Birthday Party
Horrid Henry's Holiday
Horrid Henry's Underpants

Contents

Chapter 1

Horrid Henry loved money.

He loved counting money.

He loved holding money.

He loved spending money.

There was only one problem.
Horrid Henry never had any money.

He sat on his bedroom floor and rattled his empty skeleton bank. How his mean parents expected him to get by on 50p a week pocket money he would never know.

It was so unfair!

Why should they have all the money when there were so many things *he* needed?

Comic books.

Whopper chocolate bars.

A new football.

More knights for his castle.

Horrid Henry looked round his room, scowling. True, his shelves were filled with toys, but nothing he still wanted to play with.

"If you have something to say come downstairs and say it," shouted Mum.

"I need more pocket money," said Henry. "Ralph gets a pound a week."

"Different children get different amounts," said Mum. "I think 50p a week is perfectly adequate."
"Well I don't," said Henry.

"I'm very happy with *my* pocket money, Mum," said Perfect Peter. "I always save loads from my 30p. After all, if you look after the pennies the pounds will look after themselves."

"Quite right, Peter," said Mum,
smiling.

Henry walked slowly past Peter.
When Mum wasn't looking he
reached out and grabbed him.
He was a giant crab crushing
a prawn in its claws.

"OWWW!

Henry pinched me!"

"I did not," said Henry.

"No pocket money for a week,
Henry," said Mum.

"That's not fair!" howled Henry.
"I need money!"

"You'll just have to save more,"
said Mum.
"No!" shouted Henry.
He hated saving money.

"Then you'll have to find a way
to earn some," said Mum.

Chapter 2

Earn? Earn money?
Suddenly Henry had a brilliant,
fantastic idea.

"Mum, can I set up a stall and sell some stuff I don't want?"

"Like what?" said Mum.

"You know, old toys, comics, games, things I don't use any more," said Henry.

Mum hesitated for a moment. She couldn't think of anything wrong with selling off old junk. "All right," said Mum.

"Can I help, Henry?" said Peter.

"No way,"

said Henry.

"Oh please,"

said Peter.

Don't be horrid, Henry.

"Let Peter help you," said Mum,
"or no stall."
"OK," said Henry, scowling,
"you can make the For Sale signs."

Chapter 3

Horrid Henry ran to his bedroom
and piled his unwanted jumble into
a box. He cleared his shelves of
books, his wardrobe of party clothes,
and his toy-box of puzzles with
pieces missing.

Then Horrid Henry paused.

To make

big
money

he definitely needed a few

more valuable
items.

Now, where to find some?

Henry crept into Peter's room.

He could
sell Peter's
stamp
collection,

or his nature kit.

Nah, thought Horrid Henry,
no one would want that boring stuff.

Then Henry glanced inside Mum
and Dad's room.

It was **packed** with rich
pickings.

Henry sauntered over to Mum's
dressing table. Look at all that
perfume, thought Henry.
She wouldn't miss one bottle.
He chose a large crystal one with
a swan-shaped stopper and packed
it in the box.

Now, what other jumble
could he find?

Aha! There was Dad's tennis racquet.
Dad never played tennis. That racquet
was just lying there collecting dust
when it could go to a much better
home.

Perfect, thought Henry, adding the racquet to his collection. Then he staggered out to the pavement to set up the display.

Chapter 4

Horrid Henry surveyed his stall.
It was piled high with great bargains.
He should make a fortune.

"But Henry," said Peter, looking up from drawing a sign, "that's Dad's tennis racquet. Are you sure he wants you to sell it?"

"Of course I'm sure, **stupid**," snapped Henry.

If only he could get rid of his horrible
brother, wouldn't life be perfect?
Then Horrid Henry looked at Peter.
What was it the Romans did with
their leftover captives?

Hmmn, he thought. He looked again.
Hmmmn, he thought.

"Peter," said Henry sweetly.
"How would you like to earn
some money?"

"Oh yes!" said Peter. "How?"

"We could sell you as a slave."

Peter thought for a moment.
"How much would I get?"

"10p," said Henry.

"Wow," said Peter. "That means I'll have £6.47p in my piggybank. Can I wear a For Sale sign?"

"Certainly," said Horrid Henry. He scribbled: For Sale £5, then placed the sign round Peter's neck.

"Now look smart," said Henry.
"I see some customers coming."

"What's going on?" said Moody
Margaret.
"Yeah, Henry, what are you doing?"
said Sour Susan.

"I'm having a jumble sale,"
said Henry. "Lots of bargains.
All the money raised will go to
a very good cause."

"What's that?" said Susan.
"Children in Need," said Henry.
I am a child and I'm certainly in
need so that's true, he thought.

Moody Margaret picked up
a punctured football.
"Bargain? This is just a lot of
old junk."
"No it isn't," said Henry. "Look. . .

puzzles,

books,

perfume,

stuffed toys,

and . . . a slave."

Moody Margaret looked up.
"I could use a good slave," said
Margaret. "I'll give you 25p for him."

"25p for an excellent slave?
He's worth at least £1.50p."

"Make a muscle, slave,"
said Moody Margaret.

Perfect Peter made a muscle.

"Hmmn," said Margaret.
"50p is my final offer."

"Done," said Horrid Henry.
Why had he never thought of selling
Peter before?

"How come I get 10p when
I cost 50p?" said Peter.

"Shopkeeper's expenses," said Henry.
"Now run along with your new
owner."

Business was brisk.

Rude Ralph bought some football cards. Sour Susan bought Best Bear and Mum's perfume. Beefy Bert bought a racing car with three wheels.

Then Aerobic Al jogged by.
"Cool racquet," he said, picking up
Dad's racquet and giving it a few
swings. "How much?"
"£10," said Henry.
"I'll give you £2," said Al.

£2!

That was more money than Horrid Henry had ever had in his life!

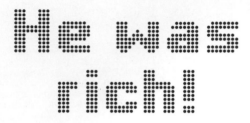

He was rich!

"Done," said Henry.

Chapter 5

Horrid Henry sat in the sitting room gazing happily at his stacks of money. £3.12p! Boy, would that buy a lot of chocolate!

Mum came into the room.

"Henry, have you seen my new perfume? You know, the one with the swan on top."

"No," said Henry.

Yikes, he never thought she would notice.

"And where's Peter?" said Mum. "I thought he was playing with you."

"He's **gone**," said Henry.

Mum stared at him.

"What do you mean, **gone**?"

"**Gone**," said Henry, popping a crisp into his mouth. "I sold him."

"You did what?"

shouted Mum. Her face was pale.

"You said I could sell anything
I didn't want, and I certainly didn't
want Peter, so I sold him to
Margaret."

Mum's jaw dropped.

"You go straight over to Margaret's and buy him back!" screamed Mum. "You horrid boy! Selling your own brother!"

"But I don't want him back," said Henry.

"No ifs or buts, Henry!" screeched Mum. "You just get your brother back."

"I can't afford to buy him," said Horrid Henry. "If you want him back you should pay for him."

"HENRY!" bellowed Mum.

"All right," grumbled Henry, getting to his feet.

Chapter 6

Henry sighed. What a waste of good money, he thought, climbing over the wall into Margaret's garden.

Margaret was lying by the
paddling pool.
"SLAVE!" she ordered.
"I'm hot! Fan me!"

Perfect Peter came out of her house
carrying a large fan.

He started to wave it in Moody
Margaret's direction.
"Faster, slave!" said Margaret.
Peter fanned faster.
"Slower, slave!" said Margaret.
Peter fanned slower.
"Slave! A cool drink, and make it
snappy!" ordered Margaret.

Horrid Henry followed Peter back
into the kitchen.
"Henry!" squeaked Peter.
"Have you come to rescue me?"

"No," said Henry.

"Please," said Peter. "I'll do anything.
You can have the 10p."

The cash register in Henry's head
started to whirl.
"Not enough," said Henry.

"I'll give you 50p.

I'll give you a pound.

I'll give you £2,"

said Peter.

"She's horrible. She's even worse than you."

"Right, you can stay here for ever,"
said Henry.

"Sorry, Henry," said Perfect Peter. "You're the best brother in the world. I'll give you all my money." Horrid Henry looked as if he were considering this offer.

"All right, wait here," said Henry. "I'll see what I can do." "Thank you, Henry," said Peter.

Horrid Henry went back into
the garden.
"Where's my drink?" said Margaret.

"My mum says I have to have Peter
back," said Henry.

Moody Margaret
gazed at him.
"Oh yeah?"

"Yeah,"

said Henry.

"Well I don't want to sell him,"
said Margaret. "I paid good money
for him."

Henry hoped she'd forgotten that.

"OK, here's the 50p," he said.

Moody Margaret lay back
and closed her eyes.

"I haven't spent all this time and
effort training him just to get
my money back," she said.
"He's worth at least £10 now."

Slowly Henry stuck his hand back
into his pocket.
"75p and that's my final offer."

Moody Margaret knew a good deal
when she was offered one.
"OK," she said. "Give me my
money."
Reluctantly, Henry paid her.

But that still leaves over £2, thought
Henry, so I'm well ahead.
Then he went in to fetch Peter.

"You cost me £6," he said.

"Thank you, Henry," said Peter.
"I'll pay you as soon as we get
home."

Yippee! thought Horrid Henry.
I'm super rich. The world is mine!

Clink, clank, clink, went Henry's
heavy pockets as Henry did his
money dance.

"CLINK, CLANK, CLINK,
I'm rich, I'm rich, I'm rich,
I'm rich as I can be,"
sang Henry.

Spend, spend, spend would be his
motto from now on.

"Hello everybody," called Dad,
coming through the front door.
"What a lovely afternoon!
Anyone for tennis?"

More HORRID HENRY

Colour books

Horrid Henry's Big Bad Book
Horrid Henry's Wicked Ways
Horrid Henry's Evil Enemies
Horrid Henry Rules the World
Horrid Henry's House of Horrors
Horrid Henry's Dreadful Deeds

Activity Books

Horrid Henry's Brainbusters
Horrid Henry's Headscratchers
Horrid Henry's Mindbenders
Horrid Henry's Colouring Book
Horrid Henry's Puzzle Book
Horrid Henry's Sticker Book
Horrid Henry's Mad Mazes
Horrid Henry's Wicked Wordsearches
Horrid Henry's Crazy Crosswords
Horrid Henry's Classroom Chaos
Horrid Henry's Holiday Havoc
Horrid Henry Runs Riot

Utterly wicked.
Totally brilliant.

Meet Henry the toddler.
Find out what happened to him
when his little brother Peter was born,
how hard he tried to get rid of him
and how he became
Henry the hero despite himself.

HORRiD
HENRY'S Illustrated
by Tony Ross
Birthday Party

Francesca Simon

EARLY READER

Utterly wicked.
Totally brilliant.

Henry can't wait for his birthday.
His parents are dreading it!
Every year his parties end in
mischief and disaster. This year,
Mum and Dad have a cunning plan.
But so does Horrid Henry!

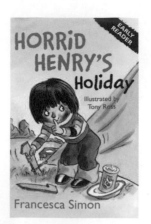

HORRiD
HENRY'S
Holiday

Illustrated by
Tony Ross

EARLY
READER

Francesca Simon

Utterly wicked.
Totally brilliant.

Henry HATES holidays. He would rather
stay at home and watch TV. But he likes
the idea of a camping trip.
The journey isn't at all what he expects
– and neither is the campsite!
It's going to be a disaster . . .

HORRID
HENRY'S
Underpants

EARLY
READER

Illustrated by
Tony Ross

Francesca Simon

utterly wicked.
Totally brilliant.

When Henry receives an
unexpected package, he is NOT
impressed to find a hideous pair
of frilly pink pants inside.
He's got to get rid of them –
and quickly!